I0706234

Pchit / Emerse

Lareina Abbott

Pchit / Emerse

Radical Bookshop and Press
4838 Richard Road SW, Suite 300
Calgary, AB T3E 6L1

FIC029000 - Fiction, Short Stories

June 1, 2024

Editor: Charlotte Hayes-Clemens
Cover Design: Lexie Angelo

Typeset in Bookmania

ISBN-13: 978-1-990201-19-6

Printed in the United States

To Jason,

*I promise the royalties will fund that sailboat
you always wanted and make up for all the
proofreading you've done over the years.*

contents

Acknowledgements

About the Author

Pchit–Little One

My name is Francine, but no-one calls me that. My
auntie calls me Pchit—little one—or Wezoo—bird. The
others don't call me anything.

Right now I am washing dishes. I need a stool, and I
can barely reach the tap to turn it on. If I don't do this job
I get in trouble, and there are others to do as well. They
are my jobs; older sister is too busy feeding the men who
pay to live at our home. They are working in the mines,
and when they come home they smell of coal and grease.

I am silent as I do the dishes. The men scare me; they
are loud and dark. I hear them in the living room, their
laughter getting louder with the beer they drink.

Mother is in the bedroom; she is not well. Father died
last year, and slowly she has been disappearing, not
gently, but like a river dropping down into a sinkhole, full
of turmoil. She might be going away, but then who will
take care of us? I don't know.

My dishes are done for now. I take the waste water
bucket from under the sink and lift it with two hands. It is
heavy. I have used too much water. I look to make sure no
one has noticed. Older sister is too busy cooking bannock
and stew for dinner. Pretty sister is sitting lazily at the
kitchen table. She has yellow hair and pouts because she
is bored. My hair is short and black; no-one thinks that I
am pretty.

I grab the bucket tighter and go out the front door. The
wooden steps were built by my father. He only had one
eye, but he could still build things. Mama told me once

10

that he had a mink farm, but then the mink all died of disease and that was the end of that.

Now that I am outside I am less careful, and the water slops over the edge. I need to dump it at the edge of the forest.

The dark trees loom on a slope above the back of our little house. They are tall and thin, dark blue shadows under deep green needles. It scares me, in there, and my heart quickens. I pass the garden, hurriedly dump the water into the bushes on the edge and run back to the stairs.

There are men walking along the dirt road in front of the house and I stop to watch. They are coming from the pulp mill. I look over and see the smoke rising from the mill. It is always rising. I sit on the steps and one of the men waves at me. I just look at him and he shrugs and keeps walking.

I hear the door creak open and I jump up but it is too late, already Mother has my ear in a pinch. She hauls me up and I trip on the step. "Kihtimiw." Lazy, she calls me, and she slaps me across the head and I fall, covering my head with my hands. I lay there. Poor me, I feel pitiful, no-one cares. *Nobody likes me, everybody hates me, guess I'll go eat worms.* The song plays in my head.

Mother does not look okay. I make my body get up and I follow her in. I glance at the forest as I go.

Later, when everyone has eaten, there is a lull. No-one has asked me to do anything and I sneak out the front door. I run down the road to the rock, the one that looks gold as the sun is going down. She is there and my heart leaps. My best friend. We hug and pick the rosehips that grow in bushes beside the rock. The bitter fruit stings our mouths, tart and sharp.

She sees the mark on my face. "It's not her fault..." I say, "she's sick." My friend nods and we say nothing.

"C'mon, I want to show you something." My friend grabs my hand and pulls me across the dirt road and down behind her house. She is pulling me to the forest. I let go.

"NO," I say. I am scared. The sky is darkening.

"C'mon," she says, insistently, but I am stubborn. My face hurts still. I stand there for a minute, my friend impatient. I look at my shoes. One heel is flapping on the bottom and I have lost the laces on the other. I am hungry. I forgot to grab some food. I am scared. My friend is frowning at me.

I look up and then I see something. A light shadow flitting across the hill, deep in the trees. Mama has told me about angels. We are Catholic. Maybe it is that. I want to see. I am scared but curious. My friend holds out her hand. I take it, and we walk in.

The air is cooler, I don't have my jacket, but my friend puts her arms round my shoulder. The pine needles blanket the ground in softness. Evening light still filters in patches through the trees. We have entered another world. There is something in here. My body tingles, but when I look at my friend she notices nothing. She pulls me up the slope. Bushes get in our way, but farther up she stops and points. An eagle's nest lies in a tree that is higher than the other trees. My heart soars. Eagles. Sometimes I see them float on the air in slow circles, up and up. I close my eyes and imagine floating with them, my house far below, the mountains surrounding us covered in pine, the crisp air, the river carrying away the melted snow.

When I open my eyes, my friend is gone. I am scared.
My heart thump-thumps in my chest. I spin, looking, but
she is nowhere.

I look up into the branches and I see an eagle, serious
and dangerous. It jumps to the edge of its nest and sits
heavily, thinking, then launches its massive body towards
me with a shriek. I run, but it catches me, and lifts me up
and up. It holds me by my ragged shirt and we fly up into
the forest, farther away from what I know. It carries me
to a rocky hilltop and dumps me. I am crying and scared
and I curl into a ball. Then I hear a voice.

"Pchit."

It is a woman. She looks like my mother but she is
fatter, and calm, not skinny and angry like my mother.
She opens her arms and I go to her, and I lie in her lap.
She strokes my hair and tells me a story. She is my
kookum, my grandmother, or maybe my grandmother's
grandmother. When she was a little girl she was lost in
the woods for two nights. A fox found her and brought
her back to the camp. She was scared of the trees too,
then.

She strokes my face and the stinging stops. She laughs
like a crow and her face crunches into lines. I trace one of
them with a finger. I nuzzle into her and she sings to me,
drumming the beat on my back. I fall asleep to the drum,
boom, ba-boom, boom. "You are brave, my little bird," I
hear her say.

When I wake I am alone on the rock. Sadness erupts
in me and I crouch and hug my knees. She has left me
a present: a feather, long and soft and dark. I take it and
tuck it into my shirt, in the sleeve, and climb down into
the forest. A path opens for me as I walk down the hill,
the moss light green and soft in the dusk.

I hear my friend yelling for me at the edge of the forest.
I run to her.

"Where were you?"

I shrug and show her the feather. Her eyes grow big.
She almost touches it but doesn't.

We run back. It is late. I will be in trouble. That is okay.
I have my feather. We hug in the road, each running to
our house in the dark.

At the house there is a car. My mother is going away.
She needs rest, they say. My sister is in charge and
sometimes my aunt will visit. Someone pats me on the
head.

I crouch in the yard, and as the car drives away I wave
to my mother. She looks at me then looks away. I put
down my hand. Maybe, where she is going, she will find
her own feather.

Emerse

The taxi narrowly missed me as I ran across the street, splashing a sludge of dirty water onto my legs. I stopped when I reached the sidewalk, felt a drip on my cheek and looked up, and remembered, too late, that you're never supposed to look up with an open mouth. A drop of rust-water fell from a metal scaffolding into my open maw. I tasted grease, dirt, exhaust—all in that little drop. I spat it out, like I wanted to spit out this city.

I was from northern British Columbia, where one could feel the light come and go like it was your own breath, where the snow didn't sit on brown piles on the sides of the road caked with car-mud and city-dirt.

"Go to the city," my uncle had said, "that's where you'll make it as a photographer. Go to Edmonton." My aunties told me to stay, stay where I had family, where I could be free, but I didn't listen to them; I wanted adventure. And now here I was, wishing for something different. I didn't want to go back to the north, but I wanted... something, something other than the skyscrapers and the dirty streets and the feeling that I could never leave. No-one had told me that being obviously Indigenous in the city meant that security guards would follow me in the supermarket to make sure I wasn't stealing anything, and that I would get called slurs by the thick, leaning men at the outdoor patios of the pubs as I walked along Whyte Ave. Being Métis in this city felt like being a stone in a blender: tough but constantly pummeled.

I raced down the sidewalk. The couple that had hired me to do their engagement photos were likely already at the hotel, and I was late. I'd slept through my alarm and eventually emerged from a heavy dream where I was held deep under lake water by long tentacles of green algae, slowly losing my breath in the dull, lifeless muck. I awoke heavy, longing for some freedom I didn't even know.

The Fairmont Hotel Macdonald was an obvious choice for a photo shoot, with its arching limestone walls, high ceilings and river valley view. I kept a hand on my camera bag as I ran. My regular trusty digital camera was in my backpack, but I also had my new find: an old film Minolta. It had no touchscreen, no automatic focus—there was only the viewfinder and me. I couldn't wait to try it. I could feel its metal heft weighing down my camera bag, solid and real.

I jogged across the road and around the corner, where my assistant Stuart stood sourly in front of the hotel. It was not a nice day, there was a chill and the light was dull, but thankfully it wasn't raining yet. The couple stood beside him. She had on a white fuzzy cashmere sweater; a big gold heart pendant sat heavy and thick like a weight around her neck. He wore dark jeans and a navy-blue wool blazer and white shirt, hair slicked back.

"I'll be right there!" I yelled needlessly as I jogged up. "Okay! Great to see you guys. Let's get started. Is everyone fed and watered? Yeah? Okay, go in and start with some close shots by the arches while we're fresh."

The Macdonald was an old Canadian Pacific Railway hotel that overlooked the river, built in 1915 to cater to rich Europeans as they rode the rails across Canada. The building blocked the view of the river valley from the street. It didn't seem fair that to get a good view of the

valley you had to pay to stay at the hotel. I thought about
how the banks of the North Saskatchewan River, where
the city now stood, was Métis farmland, before it was
taken away to serve the settlers. I probably kept coming
back here because old maps showed that my ancestors
lived on this particular rectangle of land. I imagined what
it must have been like, riding the rivers, working the
farms, getting together with kin to play music for kitchen
parties, harvesting the riches of the bushes. I wondered
what the land would be like now, if no-one had taken it
away from us.

"Ahem! Angie!" Stuart poked me, a little too hard. "Let's
get going here!"

"Okay, yeah!" I focussed my attention back on the
couple. "Let's get you standing right in the centre there
under the arch, beside each other. Great. Stuart, the
lights please? Thanks. Great. Now hold her belly like
you're really proud. Just kidding, haha. Good, good.
Perfect."

I ran through the typical first shots without thinking. I
had been here for a year. I had made it. This was what I
came here to do. Usually, I just did my job and got on with
it, but today, for some reason, each shot felt cumbersome.
Was I going to be stuck here, forever? The thought made
me want to swim to the surface, to come up for air.

"Okay, Sue and Thomas, if I could get you leaning
against that pillar right there, one of you on each side."

I kept shooting like a robot. There was no art to this
anymore.

"I'm going to switch cameras so you can just relax for a
second while I set up."

I was itching to give the Minolta a try. I couldn't believe
my luck when I'd found it sitting in a pile of obsolete

20

digital cameras in the corner of the shop. Now, I took it out, put the worn leather strap around my neck and felt the cool, heavy, tangible metal against my hands. I slid the film out of the canister and loaded it, advancing the film manually with my thumb. A giddy rush of blood ran to my head.

We walked out to the back of the hotel where a terrace looked out onto the North Saskatchewan River Valley. The river was my favourite part of the city—if only I could take the river, without the city. I looked up, darker clouds rolled against lighter ones with the threat of rain. I had to hurry.

"Let's keep going. If you could stand in the middle of the courtyard right there, I'll get some pics with the hotel in the background."

This picture was always a crowd-pleaser: it made anyone in the shot look rich and it was often the photo the couple would blow up and frame to put in their living room. I held the viewfinder up to my eye and reached around to focus manually.

I blinked to adjust my eyes to an unfamiliar scene. The light coming through the viewfinder was dramatically different than what I expected. The sun shone down from a clear blue sky and I felt my skin warm. The bright green leaves of the cottonwoods sparkled in front of me, and I could smell fresh grass. A rosehip bush prickled my side and I heard a twig snap as I shifted my weight. Sue and Thomas had disappeared from sight, along with the hotel and the city. My insides wrenched with longing.

I dropped the camera and stepped back with a sharp intake of breath. Sue and Thomas were looking at me expectantly from the grey courtyard and Stuart had one eyebrow raised quizzically. I tried to slow my heartbeat.

"Um, just getting the shot right, okay, great, let me try that again. This time, um, could you look at each other, holding both hands together? Look like you're in love."

What had just happened? I looked at the camera, turning it over. It looked like a normal old camera. I held the viewfinder up to my eye again. The warm breeze tickled my nose and I breathed in the scent of the nearby water. Ducks were calling in the background. Behind the cottonwoods rose short grassy hills, beckoning for a stroll. It was midmorning. A couple of dark-haired women with woven baskets and wearing cotton dresses picked berries in a thicket of bushes where the doors going into the hotel should have been. A farmhouse with a yard full of chickens and sheep sat solid behind them. I was looking at this hill before the hotel was built. I was looking at the land of my ancestors. My heart lurched like a car running out of gas. I brought the camera down reluctantly.

"Great job, guys. I got a few good ones there." What the hell was going on?

"Let's get you on the other side of the courtyard, right against that stone railing."

The couple lumbered over to the railing. I looked at the camera again, closer this time. All the regular parts, ISO, on/off, focus, aperture, emerse. Emerse? What did an "emerse" button do? Emerse meant to emerge, to come up out of. What use did it have on a camera? My finger hovered over the button.

Stuart hurried over, smiling tightly. "Um, Angie, what's going on? You're acting unprofessional."

"Uh, I got this new camera and..." I didn't know what to say. He was right, I was being unprofessional, but I wasn't sure if I cared anymore.

"Sure, well, whatever, just get your shots and let's get out of here. I gotta get to the mall. Easter, ya know."

"Yeah, let's get it done."

I felt a few raindrops on my head. Sue and Thomas were still at the stone railing, waiting for me to say something, to do something, to get on with it. Sue was rumpled, and Thomas ran his hand through his hair, glancing at the threatening sky. They looked like they were tired of remembering to smile. They deserved better, this was an important moment for them, but all I could think of was the river, the cottonwoods, the smell of the grass, the light, the sun, the warmth. My chest ached. What would I be going back to while Stuart was Easter shopping? A dark grey room, peeling wallpaper, a computer, my bed. It had been harder and harder to get out of bed lately. I didn't want to go to my apartment, and I didn't want to go back north to my childhood home. I wanted something real.

Stuart walked back to the lights, shooting me a scathing glance that said, "Stop being weird."

"Sue, Thomas, this is the money shot," I said.

I saw them perk up.

I looked at the camera, took a big breath in, held it tight, and brought it up to my eyes. The river reflected the sun invitingly. The slope of the hill continued to the rocky bank where ducks and geese swam in groups. I felt the stiffness in my knuckles ease. It was a lazy summer day. I kept the camera to my eye.

"Angie? Angie?" I heard Stuart walking over. "It's starting to rain! They can't hold the pose much longer." His voice rose in panic. "C'mon what are you doing?"

I knew that I was about to be drowned in dirty city rain. I didn't let go of the camera. Through the viewfinder, a man wearing a wool voyageur tunic, a belt and tights

23

walked up from the river bank towards me and waved. This man knew me. I pointed the camera down to the river behind him. A tent sat on the grass near a canoe and the remnants of a fire. The river moved like a jigger on the dance floor, calling for me to join. My right thumb reached down to the lower back of the camera, feeling for the rough button. Emerse.

If I went there, if I could go there, I may never get to touch a camera again.

"Angie, for god's sake, get your act together and finish this shoot."

My finger wavered, but only for a second. I was ready to break free. Emerse. I took a deep breath, and pressed.

ACKNOWLEDGEMENTS

Thank you to all past and present members of my Rockets to Runes writing group, to the Alexandra Writers Centre in Calgary, to the Audible Indigenous Writers Circle, and to my family, Jason and Zoe.

ABOUT THE AUTHOR

Lareina Abbott pens Métis themed speculative fiction, essays and memoir. Her stories have a tie to the spiritual and natural world. She received the 2023 Howard O'Hagan Award for her short story *Ma Soeur Marie* and is an alumni member of the Audible Indigenous Writers Circle. She originates from a cattle ranch in northern British Columbia but lives and writes in Calgary.